ANGELS AND MYSTERIES

AND INCREDIBLE HAPPENINGS IN THE WILD WILD WEST

Angels and Mysteries
and Incredible Happenings in the Wild Wild West

IRV LAMPMAN

ReadersMagnet, LLC

Angels and Mysteries and Incredible Happenings in the Wild Wild West
Copyright © 2021 by Irv Lampman. All rights reserved.

Published in the United States of America

ISBN Paperback: 978-1-954371-63-7
ISBN Hardback: 978-1-958030-11-0
ISBN eBook: 978-1-954371-62-0

All rights reserved. No part of this publication may be reproduced, stored in a retrieval system or transmitted in any way by any means, electronic, mechanical, photocopy, recording or otherwise without the prior permission of the author except as provided by USA copyright law.

The opinions expressed by the author are not necessarily those of ReadersMagnet, LLC.

ReadersMagnet, LLC
10620 Treena Street, Suite 230 | San Diego, California, 92131 USA
1.619.354.2643 | www.readersmagnet.com

Book design copyright © 2021 by ReadersMagnet, LLC. All rights reserved.
Cover design by Ericka Obando
Interior design by Mary Mae Romero

Table of Contents

Dedications vii

The Days of the Wild West 1
Preamble to: My Helper and our Guardian 2
The Indian Attack That Wasn't 7
Preamble to: Cave in at the Lucky 7 8
Preamble to: The Visitors 10
Preamble to: Angels at the Alamo. 12
The Doctor's Unbelievable Trip 13
Great Fire in Deadwood. 15
Disease 17
Cholera. 18
Preamble to: Raiders 20
Preamble to: Unlikely Angel 22
The Miracle at the Orphanage 24
A Warning that Went Unheeded 25
The Hanging of Jose Garcia 27
Preamble to: The Old Man's Winter Night Visitor 29
Strange Happenings on the Trail Dodge / Ghost herd 31
Preamble to: The Men with the Tied Down Guns 33
The Last Citizen of Dry Creek. 35
The Unbelievable Prediction of Crazy Horse 36
The Legend of Colter's Hell 37
The Tale of the Walker - Bennesh Wagon Train and the Desert Crossing. 38
The Saving of Boonesborough 40
The Legend of Wyatt Earp: The Man No Bullet Could Kill 41

Geronimo: The Businessman 42
The Wrong Man, The Mystery of the Death of Billy the Kid. 43
Old Guzzler 44
The Speech of Chief Logan 45
Abilene Kansas, "Hell Has Laid Its Egg and at Abilene it Hatched" 46
The Wonderful Christmas Story in Wyoming 1891 47
The Mystery of the Dodge City Stage 48
Marshall Taylor's Last Day. 49
Lion 51
When the Buffalo Came Back 55

DEDICATIONS

First off let me say this book is dedicated to the world's greatest parents Orlin and Dorothy Lampman.

To Helen and Jim Vest, our best friends who got us married on the mountain in Tennessee.

To Sandy, who brightens my day with her smiles, a wonderful wife.

To Dave Friske who you can count on to ride the river with even when the boats leakin'.

To Winston Whitford, thanks for a lifetime of friendship.

And to my brother Don who died in a car accident in 62', gone but never forgotten!

The Days of the Wild West

During the western expansion of the United State what is generally referred to as the Wild West. Sometimes things happened that defy man's ability to explain or understand. During the hardest times someone or something intervened. Some people would say it was angels. In case of the Jose Garcia, when man was about to make a grievous mistake, someone would say an angel intervened. Time and time again when they were most needed, the Lord sent some of his emissaries to help.

Most of these stories were told to me by an old lady who was born at the end of the Civil War and grew up in the time of Billy the Kid, Wyatt Earp and Doc Holiday, the cattle drives and the wagon trains headed west. If you could have looked in those tired old eyes as I did, you would have taken what she had to say as gospel. What you choose to believe my friends is up to you!

Preamble to: My Helper and our Guardian

Sometimes in the Wild West, when all seemed lost, someone was sent to help, so in the case of my helper and our guardian.

My Helper and our Guardian

One of the greatest fears of people in the west, which during the 1870's was what we called the Wild, was desolation. People had to go to town for supplies. Someone had to stay home to feed the cattle, hogs and chicken. And the cows had to be milked and stored. It was stored away in the springhouse where it could stay cool and not sour.

This is a story told to me by an old lady that swore absolutely true. If you could have looked into those old eyes, you could believe it just like I did. This is about a family called the Warrens.

One particular morning Mr. Warren had saddled up early to go to town for supplies. He wanted to get an early start so he could be home by dark. He buckled a belt full of cartridges around his waist from which hung a Colts revolver. He put a rifle in the saddle boot, kissed his wife goodbye and rode off for town. The day dragged on, out there on the prairie. There was not much to do during the day; Ms. Warren did have a couple of books that she had read until the covers wore off. Along about four o'clock, she put some potatoes and carrots in a pot to boil and when they were done, she set them aside and went out to the barn to do chores. She had brought a beef roast from the springhouse and put it in the pot with the potatoes and carrots and put them in the coals in the fireplace to cook. She walked out on the porch of the cabin and cast anxious eyes toward town, watching for her husband. She expected him before this, but anything could have delayed him.

At nine o'clock, she put their two children to bed and blew out the lantern. She sat with her back to the wall and a double barrel shotgun within easy reach on the table before her. By the next morning, she knew something was terribly wrong. In those days, any number of things could have happened. The horse could have stepped in a prairie dog hole, a snakebite at a stream and waterhole. Indians were still a problem and outlaws infested the roads that traveled across this land. She was not too surprised when she saw the sheriff and the doctor's buggy approaching sometime after sun up.

The sheriff pulled up and Mrs. Warren asked the men in, *"Well Sheriff, Doctor… What happened?"*

"Well Mrs. Warren, your husband's been badly hurt. He's alive but he's in pretty bad shape."

"Well was he shot or ran off the road, or what?"

"We really don't know." He has been beaten terribly. One of the ranchers and his wife was coming from town and happened to see his horse standing under a tree and went to check on it. They went back into town to get the sheriff and me!

"Well, I'll get the kids ready and we'll come into town! Oh, I forgot. I can't come until I can find somebody to look after the place!"

"Well, no need for that Ms. Warren. I will bring him as soon as he is well enough to travel! In the meantime, you'd better get some rest. You look like you had a rough night."

"I did! I knew something was wrong!"

"Mrs. Warren, do you know who would do this? Did your husband have trouble with somebody? Well, somebody either tried to kill him because he was mad about something or tried to rob him! Your husband have a lot of money on him?"

"Hardly. You don't make a lot of money in a place like this. Not enough that somebody would want to attack somebody for!"

"Well, I'll ask around and see if somebody might want a job for a few days so you can get into town to see your husband. In the meantime, try not to worry."

The doctor said, *"If he gets plenty of rest he'll be all right. But it's not gonna happen overnight!"*

"We can't afford to pay anybody much!"

"Well, let's see what I can do!"

After the men left Mrs. Warren got the kids ready for the day and went out to do chores. As she went out to the barn, she was startled by a man at the horse trough. Both the man and his horse looked the worse for wear. Mrs. Warren couldn't help noticing the gun slung low on his hip.

"What do you want?" The frightened woman asked.

"Why, only to water my horse and get a drink myself. It's gonna be a hot day for both man and beast. May I have a little of your water?"

"Of course, you just help yourself."

"Thank you very much! Can I do anything to help you Ma'am?"

"No, we're doing alright. Just refresh yourself and then be on your way!"

Mrs. Warren went into the barn to milk Bossy, as she called the cow. She had just finished and pitched some hay when she heard some hoof beats coming up the path from the road. When she stepped out into the sunlight, she saw she had some more visitors. But these men were much more unsavory types. They were unshaven and their clothes were so dusty they looked like they hadn't been washed in weeks.

"Well hello. What have we here?" the man she took to be the leader said with a lecherous grin.

"What do you want, we have no money!"

"Well, all we wanted was a little food and water for our horses! But there's no need to be in a hurry!"

Mrs. Warren ran for the house. If she could just reach the shotgun, she thought she might have a chance, but the man moved like lightening to cut her off from the house and grabbed her, pulling her to him. The smell of his liquor soaked breath made her face feel like she might faint.

"Let her go!" came a commanding voice from the corner of the house!

"Who the hell are you?" the outlaw said.

"Let's just say somebody who don't like a skunk like you manhandling a decent woman!"

"Mighty big talk when there's four of us and only one of you!"

The outlaw's hands flashed for their guns then froze. The stranger's gun was in his hand and the hammer was back. The leader of the prairie outlaws always thought of himself as a fast gun. He hadn't even seen the strangers hand move, but there was the gun, the muzzle looking like the gates of hell!

"Now I think it would be best if you fellas just watered your horses and then moved on don't you?"

The outlaws got their horses watered and filled their canteens and then left in a hurry!

"How can I ever thank you?" Mrs. Warren asked.

"Oh, there's no need for that! Just take care of yourself and your children. Say, where's your husband, you're not out here all alone on this place are you?"

Mrs. Warren explained what the doctor had said had happened to her husband.

"Well, why don't you get the kids and take the buckboard to town. I can look after things for you for a couple of days. I know it would make you and your husband feel better and I know the kids want to see their dad!"

Mrs. Warren said she really didn't know why she trusted the man, a stranger to look after her ranch. But she did, something told her that he could be trusted.

She got the kids ready and headed for town. She was shocked to see how badly injured her husband really was. He lay on the bed in the doctor's office barely able to move! After a nice visit as it was approaching sundown she made up her mind to spend the night with a family her and her husband were friendly with. The woman lost her husband to a snakebite a couple of years ago, and Mrs. Warren knew she'd enjoy the company. The women had a nice visit. Mrs. Warren happened to mention the dusty stranger who had happened to show up at her place and saved her from a very unpleasant experience.

"Are you sure you can trust this man. Don't you think it's kinda funny, him showing up just when you needed him the worst?"

"Yes, I do. I don't know why, but I do! He didn't have to face those prairie skunks for me, but he did! He didn't have to watch the place for me, but he offered to and I accepted. If it wasn't for him, I couldn't have left the place to come in here to see my husband. He is a gunman, he drew his guns so fast he could have killed all four of them, but he didn't. I don't know who he is, but he is a good man. I've no doubt about that!"

"Well I certainly hope so. There's no way of knowing what kind of men are roaming the west out there on the plains!"

After a good night's sleep, Mrs. Warren stopped to see her husband and then headed back to the ranch. She arrived 3 p.m. There was wood in the wood box for cooking. The pigs, chickens and the cattle had been fed. The only thing left to do was milk the cows and put the milk in the springhouse. Mrs. Warren fed the horse that had pulled the buckboard from town and made sure he had water. There was no sign of her helper. However, she knew he was around! That night as the fire burned low and she and the children turned in for the night, she could feel that someone was watching over them.

The next morning when she went out to the barn, the animals had been fed, the barn cleaned, the cows had been milked and the milk was in the springhouse. Incredibly not a sound had disturbed the families sleep. That afternoon, an Indian warrior stopped at her gate asking for some food and water. She gave it to the warrior and watched while he had his meal!

"You are the woman who is protected by the above one!" he said.

"The medicine man says you are protected by the above one and it will be bad for the tribe if you are harmed!" The warrior said. *"You need have no fear of any Redman. We will watch over you as long as your family lives here!"*

"Tell your Chief, your people can always stop here for water. The above one will be pleased that you make us welcome in your hunting grounds."

For better than a month it was the same, there was help with the chores when she needed it. No other outlaws came near the place. After the word got out, the unsavory characters gave the ranch a wide berth.

Mr. Warren at last made it home and the doctor said he'd check every few days to make sure Mr. Warren's recovery continued. Whoever their benefactor was, they never seen him again. No trace of him was seen in town, no trace along the trails and the Sheriff hadn't found anyone who had ever seen him.

However, one thing had been seen. One of the ranchers on his way from town had seen a huge white light hovering the sky over the hills above the ranch. It seems the above one felt the Warrens could now take care of themselves and the helper and guardian was no longer needed.

The Indian Attack That Wasn't

In the history of the Wild West, there is one story that stands out as one of the stories of angels; which stands out to this day. There was an Indian tribe that was famous as terrible fighters. No other tribe could match them for ferocity. All the tribes in the Wild West had met them in battle and had learned to fear them as no other.

The soldiers that had ventured into their land had fought them and after suffering heavy casualties, the white man had holed up in a fort but expected that sooner or later they would be overwhelmed and wiped out.

Suddenly one morning, the hills around the fort came alive with Indians. But as the soldiers prepared themselves for death, they noticed that the warriors carried their weapons out in front of them. This was a sign of surrender. Not one shot was fired. Not a war hoop sounded. The Chief came forward with his weapons out in front of him and when a group of soldiers ventured out to meet him, he told his story.

"We have never known fear. We have fought all the tribes of the plains and defeated them all. If we wished to, we could destroy the white man and all his forts and homes until there was nothing left. But the night before last in our stronghold suddenly over our village appeared a huge shining cloud. Out of the cloud came a group of shining beings. Their clothing was like shining beams. Their hair and beard shone like fine wool. They told us to put down our weapons and to make war no more. They told us that if we did make war, all people and villages would be destroyed and blown away on the wind. They said we must learn to live in peace, with the whites. This was commanded by the Great Spirit creator of all things. We bring our weapons to the soldiers only keeping what we need for hunting. We ask that you show us how to make the land bring forth growing things to feed our families. We will make war no more!"

This tribe has remained peaceful to this day. They raised sheep and goats. They make jewelry out of colored stones, woven clothing and blankets from the wool. Now, if you believe this story of the visitors to this mighty warrior tribe or not, the fact is they came in peace, laid down their weapons and never made war again. What could cause such a change, only angels. There can be no other explanation.

Preamble to: Cave in at the Lucky 7

Mining in the west was a very dangerous profession. Cave-ins were common, mines could be flooded out. Most of the time there were no warnings. But in this case of the Lucky 7, a warning was given that without a doubt saved lives. Heavenly visitors arrived almost at the minute when the cave-in happened.

Cave in at the Lucky 7

In the days of the Wild West, two things caused more gunfights than anything, greed and gambling, followed by whiskey and women. In the case of tombstone, it was silver. Ed Shefline happened to tell an army sergeant that he was going into the mountains to prospect. The sergeant laughed and said, "All you'll find there is your tombstone." Shefline went anyway and made the greatest silver strike in Arizona history. So it followed that the town that sprang up would be named Tombstone.

The mountains around the town were soon honeycombed with mines and tunnels. Prospectors drilled holes, tunnels, and large mines all with the purpose of striking it rich. One such mine was named the Lucky 7, because the current owner had won it in a card game. He soon realized that he had something. The ore assayed out as very rich. He brought in equipment and began to mine in earnest. However, the former owner wasn't going to take it lying down. And when the owner wouldn't share in his good fortune as it happened so many times in the Wild West. It led to a challenge and to a gunfight.

The men met on Main Street at noon. The lucky man's luck still held and he was the fastest. Witnesses said the dead man drew first, so there was no need for inquest. The matter was dropped, however, the trouble at the Lucky 7 had just began. It was about a week later that laborers hired to work the mine reported strange rumblings coming from deep in the bowels of the earth. No one

Angels and Mysteries and Incredible Happenings in the Wild Wild West

wanted to enter the Lucky 7 until a survey of the mine was conducted. Mine experts came in from the government office in Tucson.

The results were the entire mine must have new shoring up. However, that would cost a small fortune, not to mention the delay in getting the ore out. The owner offered to pay higher wages to anyone who would agree to work the mine. Men desperate to feed their families and to make money agreed.

But the next morning when the men reported for work, three men stood blocking the entrance to the mine. The men all wore clean white clothing and it was said their beards and hair were all snow white. "You will not enter this mine. It will collapse right now. We will not allow anyone to die here!" At that very moment, a tremendous shaking of the ground under their feet began and dust and dirt poured out of the tunnel. Cave in. Had it not been for the men in white, 30 men would have died. The men who gave the warning had disappeared, never to be seen again.

When most of us think of angels, we think of the heavenly host that informed the shepherds of the savior's birth in the fields around Bethlehem. We think of the angels for example at the tomb that informed the women at the garden tomb that Jesus had risen. In the Wild West, there were happenings that defy all other explanation other than heavenly visitors, like in the case of the hanging of Jose Garcia.

Preamble to: The Visitors

These were the men who came out of the storm to help a family facing starvation. Such were the visitors I choose to believe they were angels, sent to help a family in desperate need.

The Visitors

In the days of the Wild West, there were times of extreme hardship that was sometimes almost unbearable. Pioneers faced floods, heat stroke, snakebite, savage beasts and savage men both red and white.

One such case was the Donner Party that became trapped in the mountains and had to resort to cannibalism to survive. This is the story of the Kelly Family who had lost everything, the civil war had taken two brothers; the carpetbaggers had taken their farm. Nothing was left. When they heard of land in Kansas almost for the taking, they packed up their few belongings and headed west, trusting to God and luck to get them through. They had absolutely no idea what was waiting for them.

Everything went fine for the first week. The sun came up during the day to warm them and at night they camped along a stream if there was one. All in all, it seemed to be a great adventure they had embarked upon, but everything changed on the 10th night out. It began to turn colder and the wind blew down from the north with a bone chilling bite that forced the mother and the younger children to ride in wagon to get some shelter from the wind. By 3:00 pm, it had begun to snow and by dark, it was impossible to go on. The shape of a cabin and a shed of sorts loomed up out of the darkness. Mrs. Kelly got the littlest children inside while the oldest boys helped their father get the horses bedded down in the shed. There was some grain on the wagon but the father knew there was not enough to last the horses for long.

They were able to get a fire going in the fireplace and with the blankets off the wagon, they managed to be at least a little comfortable. The parents awoke during the night and by the sound

Angels and Mysteries and Incredible Happenings in the Wild Wild West

of the wind, they knew they were caught in a full-blown blizzard. There was bacon on the wagon, some grain for the horses and some canned food the mother had wisely brought along, but mom and dad Kelly knew they were in trouble. They could melt snow for water but for food, they'd have to kill the horses. Then when the weather improved, how would they pull the wagon?

At daylight, their worst fears were confirmed. The snow was piled up to the eves of the cabin, and the wind was blowing so hard it was impossible to see the shed where the horses were. The wind was blowing so hard it was impossible to see any break in the storm. The father burst out in desperation, *"We're in big trouble if this storm don't break! God help us! How am I going to feed all of you?"*

Just as Mr. Kelly was getting ready to see if he could fight his way out through the snow to feed the horses, a knock came on the door.

"Who in the world could be out in this storm?" the mother asked. Almost in fear, they opened the door. Three men stood there bundled in mackinaws, fur caps that looked like bear skins and warm mittens made the same way. The mother would say later that despite their rough appearance, they looked like angels standing there.

"Figured you folks could use some help. There's a quarter buffler hung up in the shed and a couple of sacks of grain of the horses. There's hay in the mow too."

"Who sent you?" the mother asked.

"Let's just say from someone that's been keeping an eye on you."

"We'll be around if you need more help. Better get some meat brought in and stay in where it's warm. "We'll bring in some wood from those oak trees over there and see to the horses!"

"How much do I owe you?" the father asked.

"Not a penny son. Just take care of your family, that's all we ask."

The family remained at the isolated farmstead for the rest of the winter. They never saw their benefactors again. Their supply of meat was replenished, as they needed it. They were always able to stay warm and they always had grain and hay for the horses.

The winter broke at the end of March. Warm winds turned around to come in from the southwest. The geese were flying in their wedges across the sky and the meadowlarks sang from the prairie grass. The family said goodbye to their unseen visitors and headed on west.

They stopped at the general store at the next town for supplies before heading west. When they asked about the men who helped them, the storekeeper said, *"Huh, must have been angels. No mortal men would have been out on the prairie in a storm like that. And another thing, where'd they get buffalo meat? There ain't been a herd through here in years!"*

The Kelly family headed on west to meet their destiny. They always believed it was angels that visited them in that terrible storm so many years before.

Preamble to: Angels at the Alamo

All of us grew up in history books and the story of the Alamo, when 179 brave men crossed the line drawn by Travis in the sand and every man died. When the cry of Remember of the Alamo echoes down through time. But there is another story that most people haven't heard of. Guardians that watch over the Alamo to this day.

Angels at the Alamo

San Antonio, Texas, March 1836

The battle was over. All the brave men who sold their lives so dearly died that Texas might live. One hundred and eighty including Bowie, Travis, Crockett and Williamson. All had been burned on a funeral fire. The Mexican general El Presedente Santa Anna had pulled out to find Huston and his rag tag army to be the north.

The next day, Santa Anna received some disturbing news. He had given orders that the Alamo was to be burned to the ground, but the men he had ordered to accomplish this task had returned and fell on their face before him. They said they had the torches lit when 4 specters came out of the Alamo's gate with pointed rifles along with them were three men in garments that were shining like the sun.

"Tell your general that the Alamo will not be burned. Not today or any day. Tell him his army will be destroyed and Texas will be free. A new country has been born and Texas will join it!"

Santa Anna dismissed the men with a wave of his hand, but the first feeling of fear chilled his heart. He had no way of knowing that the cry of *"Remember the Alamo"* would be rallying cry that would defeat him and three shining men will stand guard over the Alamo forever.

The Doctor's Unbelievable Trip

In most towns in the Wild West, there was one doctor and he did his best to cover a huge area between delivering babies, patching up knife and bullet wounds and covering any amount of accidents. At times, it was almost impossible to cover a large area so in the case of the doctor's unbelievable trip.

The Doctor's Unbelievable Trip

Apache Junction Arizona 1879

Doctors in the west were scarce at best in the days of the horse and buggy. In the days of the horse buggy, it sometimes took a day or better to reach an outlining ranch or farm, sometimes up to 2 days at which time the doctor had to camp out overnight. It was such a time when a doctor Chadwick was camped out along the base of the Superstition Mountains. He'd had a good supper of bacon and beans and after a smoke of his pipe, he'd turned in for the night. He figured to reach his destination the next day where a young lady was about due to bring a baby into the world. The doctor wanted to be sure to be there when the blessed event occurred.

It was about 3am when he was awakened by three men. The light from them shone as bright as the sun at midday.

"Doctor Chadwick, wake up. You are needed urgently at Taylor Ranch. There's been a shouting. Also, Mrs. Saunders will be in labor in the afternoon. Can we help you in any way?"

"Not unless you can get me to the Taylor Ranch immediately. I need to get to whoever needs me as quick as possible."

Suddenly the doctor found himself at the gate to the Taylor Ranch. He didn't remember traveling there, but there he was. He called out to the ranch and rang the bell at the gate. In less time than he could open the gate, he was surrounded by barking dogs.

"How did you get here so quick?" the rancher asked.

"I just sent Tommy to town to get you. He ain't been gone more than an hour."

"Well, never mind that, what happened here?"

"Oh a couple of the boys got in a fight over a card game. Dave Schultz thinks he's Wes Hardin. They grabbed their guns and Joe shot the dang fool. He's got a hole in his chest."

"Well get me to him. There's a baby ready to show up at the Saunders place this afternoon!"

"Well he's over at the Bunk House. I don't know how you can take care of Dave and get clear over to the Saunders place that quick!"

Doctor Chadwick found a man with a huge hole in his chest. He could really tell by the size of the hole it was from a forty-five. The man's breathing was labored but steady. There was a hole in the back, which showed the bullet had missed the heart and lungs by a miracle. Doctor Chadwick bound the wounds tightly. The patient moaned and moved. That was a good sign, Doc said. It showed the patient was unconscious but not in a coma.

"Well, that's about all I can do for him right now. Keep him warm and watch to see if there's any sign of infection like a bad fever. If he does get worse send to get me. I'll be over to the Saunders place. That baby ain't gonna wait forever."

After some coffee to help keep him awake the doctor started down the road to the Saunders place. Despite himself he must have drifted off. The next thing he was awake in front of a squeaking gate and dog barking.

"I told Tom he should get the hinges oiled on that gate!" he said to himself. Then he jolted awake. It was still dark. How did he get here? It was miles away from the Taylor Ranch to get here. The last thing he remembered was leaving the Taylor Ranch and yet here he was.

Mr. Saunders came out on the porch. *"Who's there?"* he called out.

Doc could see lantern light gleaming off shotgun barrels. In that day and late at night when someone came to your door unexpectedly, you carried a weapon.

"It's Doc Chadwick! You gonna put that canon down and let me come in?"

"Well yes, Doc yes come on in. Where did you come from? It's time for the baby. I sent Able to fetch you only a half hour ago!"

"Never mind that, you got coffee on?"

"Sure do, Doc, the Mrs. Will sure be glad to see you."

The new arrival at the Saunders place made her debut at 1pm that afternoon. But for years afterward, the questions continued. How did the doctor manage to cover over forty miles to treat a wounded man and then another 15 miles to welcome a new baby that afternoon on a trip that should have taken him at least 30 hours. No one knows for sure. But someone or something helped him on his trip in 1879. Angels, there is no other explanation.

Great Fire in Deadwood

One of the things that the people feared in the Wild West was fire. Most of the buildings were wooden; the equipment to fight fire in the west was non-existent, leaving the only way to fight a fire to be a bucket brigade. Many times the water supply was very limited.

In the case of Deadwood, there were three fires that almost destroyed the town. But thanks to warnings given, loss of life was minimal. Most say an angel gave warning.

Great Fire in Deadwood

From the Stories of Homer McNight

Deadwood South Dakota sprang up because of a great gold strike in the Black Hills that was really one of the major causes of the Little Big Horn defeat of George Armstrong Custer. By treaty, the Black Hills was to belong to the Sioux for as long as the grass would grow. However, when gold was found like always, the white man broke his word and sent Custer and the 7th Cavalry to drive the Sioux onto reservations, the result was Custer's last stand.

The name Deadwood was named for the huge amount of dead wood piled up in the gulch.

Any number of characters came to Deadwood hoping to strike it rich. One of them was the famous James Butler Hickock better known as Wild Bill who tried his luck at prospecting, but then that was unsuccessful turned to gambling. Buffalo Bill Cody and Martha Jane Canary better known as Calamity Jane ended up in Deadwood and spent time at the tables winning quite a lot of money.

Hickock was killed by a little weasel named Jack McCall, Calamity Jane after Hickock died, drank herself to oblivion. Buffalo Bill went on to scout for the army, killing yellow hand, the Cheyenne was chief. However, the Indians or outlaws weren't the only threat to Deadwood. Fire was the one thing all of the old western towns feared more than gunfighters. For one thing, the equipment they had to fight fires with was very inefficient. Deadwood was nearly destroyed several times by fire, not long after the death of Wild Bill Hickock. But the real story can be found in taking to the residents of the town; stories that have been handed down from generation to generation.

One such story tells of a dire warning given to the mayor's office. It said the town would be destroyed by fire. Also the sheriff was told by a stranger that showed up at his office that he'd better get all the people out of town. The stranger said that the town would burn to the ground three times. The town was nearly destroyed. By luck, the town survived and was rebuilt till again it's like a Wild West town although without the gunfights that marked its early history. Again, should the strangers not showed up to warn the town, the loss of life would have been horrendous.

So many times in the Wild West, someone or something interfered to stop a disastrous loss of life. Being a fast gun meant a man could take another man's life literally in the blink of an eye. But sometimes somebody interfered. Thank God for angels.

DISEASE

In the Wild West, death by disease came by many names, small pox, yellow fever and Cholera. Many times physicians lacked the knowledge to fight the disease. Medicine was limited so people died. Sometimes a whole town, but in one case someone intervened. No doubt, it was angels. The men who came to help had the knowledge and supplies to help. People that were there said the strangers were straight from heaven. I believe they were.

Cholera

This story comes to us in the 21st century from an old lady that wishes to remain unknown. I've agreed to her wishes.

The town was like many towns in the west. Only one doctor made his office there and he did the best he could to take care of the people that made the town home as well and the ranches in the surrounding area. Most times, he was able to handle the bullet wounds, knifings, even toothaches when the need arose. He knew he'd never get rich, but with the pay from the larger ranches and the eggs and bacon preserves and vegetables from the gardens in town; handle what needed doing, and when the time came, retire comfortably. However, he wasn't ready for what happened one Wednesday morning when a man from one of the saloons in town came running in.

"Doc, Miss Mary from the Silver Spur says she needs you to get down there right away. She's scared. She says it's a matter of life and death!"

The doctor grabbed his bag and hurried for the Silver Spur. He knew that if Mary said it was a matter of life and death, then it was.

When he got there, the saloon owner hurried them to the back room where a man lay on a cot. The man's breathing was labored and he was shaking with chills. The doctor didn't have to go very far before he knew that was ailing the young cowboy. Cholera! The doctor had seen it at a civil war camp and on one of the wagon trains that passed through the area on its way west.

In that day and age sanitation was almost unheard of. Raw sewage was sometimes dumped in the street and excrement from horses, cattle, pigs and people then especially after a rain it washed into the river, where a lot of people got their water and even into the wells of the wealthier homes and eating establishments.

Within 24 hours, nine more cases of Cholera had spread through the population. Seven more people showed signs of the disease and the next morning, 10 were dead. The doctor ordered that all the sick be separate from the people and remain isolated, but his knowledge to fight the disease was limited.

Angels and Mysteries and Incredible Happenings in the Wild Wild West

By the third day, half the population was ill and two of the outlying ranches had cases of the illness. The doctor worked until he was ready to collapse. That evening as the doctor was taking a rare break, a soft knock came on the door. When he opened it, he expected another report of more illness. Instead, four people stood in the light from his lantern.

"Doctor Owens?" they asked. There were two men and two women.

"Yes. And *who might you be?*" the doctor asked.

"We've come to lend assistance. We've heard that you have a terrible problem here!"

"I surely do. But where did you come from and how did you hear about our problem here?"

"Let's just say when something like this happens, people must pull together. We're here to help."

"Well, thank God. What do you think I should do?"

"Well, the first thing is you need to get some rest. It won't do for you to drop dead of a heart attack. Your people need you! We'll get started at what needs doing!"

"But there's so many people! How can you get to everybody even if there is four of you?"

"Never mind that doctor. Just lay down for a little while, we'll wake you up when you're needed."

The doctor laid down intending to close his eyes for only a few minutes. Low and behold, when he awakened it was nearly 9 am. His housekeeper had breakfast ready but he only took time for a cup of coffee as he hurried out the door.

The visitors who had come to help were waiting for him when he reached the street.

"Good morning Doctor. We know what we need to do. We need help getting it done!"

What can I do to help?" the doctor asked.

"First, all water has to be boiled, it's full of sickness! All clothing from the dead or dying must be burnt! All eating utensils must be boiled in hot water. You lost four more people during the night! If we want to stop this thing, that's what needs doing. Help us convince your people to do what we ask!"

"I'll do all I can, but you must realize these people are frightened. Scared people are dangerous people!"

"Well, the facts are these! This is Cholera. We know it's caused by a disease in the water and spreads from person to person. We come to help and we will no matter what."

The strangers began going from house to house. Something about these visitors reached the town folk. They knew that these visitors had come to help. No one knew where they had come from, only that they were trying to help. The cemetery on the hill welcomed twelve new visitors since the epidemic began. These visitors seemed to know what they were doing.

In this day and age, we know that the disease come from raw sewage getting into the water, streams, wells and cisterns. But in the days of the Wild West, they didn't know where death was coming from. But the oldest people remembered the strangers as angels. Angels that came to save their town. For slowly, but surely the death and disease slowed down and then stopped. Life returned to normal. One day, the strangers were gone; the doctor said he believes God himself sent these angels of mercy. I do, too.

Preamble to: Raiders

Sometimes in the Wild West, people were killed for no rhyme or reason. Men on horseback swept down on a lone homestead, killed, and then were gone leaving nothing but grief behind. At such time, someone or something came to stop the killing and bring solace to the broken hearted so in case of the raiders.

The Raiders

The raiders came one morning at sun up. Mike Hennesy had just finished his breakfast and after his second cup of coffee had started for the barn. As he stopped out on the porch, a bullet struck him dead center in the forehead and ended his earthly life forever in the Wild West. His wife heard the shot and calling to her husband, she ran out on the porch and stumbled over his body. She to fell victim to a rifle shot. Their son Joey jumped from breakfast and grabbing his father's rifle headed out the door. He found the bodies of his parents and fired at one of the murderers. Joey had grown up shooting squirrels and his aim was true. The raider fell out of the saddle with a huge hole as large as a dinner plate in his back. A bullet whistled by the boy's head. Joey saw a dark figure duck back into the barn and when the outlaw peeked out, Joey caught him dead center in the forehead with the huge bullet from the Buffalo Gun.

Joey's dog, Jumper, was barking and snarling, doing his part to help. He sank his teeth into the ankle of one of the raiders trying to get to the house. The man cursed and swung his rifle at the dog knocking him rolling. Joey screamed in anger and fired at the man who struck the dog, the heavy slug knocked the man rolling. Just then, while the fight was going on a great blinding light descended down over the farmyard. Joey would say later that everything became quiet as death. The yelling and cursing, the roar of the rifles became as silent as death. Joey would later say that four beings in blinding white robes descended from the light. The raiders fell on their faces in fear. The angels, for that was what Joey would later say they were, with a wave of their hand ordered the men out of the yard. As the raiders fell all over themselves to get out of the yard, the angels surrounded Joey to shield him from harm. One of the beings said to Joey.

"Son, you have found favor with the Lord. You have fought valiantly and honestly for your life, not for revenge. We want you to know your parents are now safe and happy together in a new world of which is not ruled by violence and killing. They will no longer feel pain, only love. However, they want you to know they will watch over you always. Jumper is with them!"

In later years, as Joey grew up and built his own life, he was always known for honesty and integrity. He never ceased to praise and thank his Lord for delivering him on the terrible day when his parents and Jumper were taken and the angels came to protect him.

Preamble to: Unlikely Angel

Sometimes in the Wild West, something would happen that caused a man to rise above his abilities. As sometimes happens, a man could become something nobody thought he was, as in the case of Orle Jenkins.

Unlikely Angel

He really didn't look like an angel, he wasn't very tall and he wasn't really that good looking. His ears were a little too big and his nose was a little too prominent. His name was Orle Jenkins. He managed to make it through the sixth grade but then he had to go to work helping his father on the family farm. But at least he could read, write, and do his sums. That was a lot more that a lot of children in that day and age could do.

The people of the town went about their daily lives just doing the best they could do to cope with the hard chore of daily living. Then one afternoon everything changed. A train coming down out of the mountains suddenly was running wild. The engineer was dead at the throttle and the train was gaining speed every 10 feet. It was loaded with explosives from the mines at the top of the mountain and there was no way to stop it. No way that is, except Orle Jenkins. The train passed him fairly flying but Orle had time to see there was no one at the throttle, and no one on top of the cars. The brake man had long since given up trying to stop the train and when the train slowed a little at a grade, had jumped off, choosing to save himself.

Orle knew that the one chance he had to stop the train was to jump aboard when it passed a place where a cottonwood limb hung over the tracks. From there, if everything went right, he should be able to drop down on top of the steam engine and reach the throttle to get the smoke belching monster to slow down.

Orle got to climb over the tracks just in time. The engine came around the curve and under the cottonwood and Orle dropped down on the roof of the cab. He grabbed the throttle back and the train began slowly slowing down. He pulled the cord to signal the brakeman but the brakeman had long since abandoned ship figuring the train was a lost cause. At last, Orle got the train slowed down and finally to a halt. The town was saved.

Orle lived all his life on the sign of his greatest accomplishment. In the cemetery is a marble monument that reads, *"Here lies Orle Jenkins who turned out to be our very own angel born on 1840 and died 1895. Had it not been for Orle, our town's history might have ended on a very hot day in 1873."*

The Miracle at the Orphanage

In the history of the Wild West on the Great Plains, there were many forces that couldn't be stopped by the possess or guns vigilantes. A force that even today with our modern knowledge we cannot control.

Tornadoes, in the Wild West, they were called twisters. In Oklahoma, Kansas and Iowa is an area called tornado alley.

In a Wild West town is a place that is dedicated to the care of children. That for any number of reasons has become orphans that had lost their parents. These unfortunate waifs have nowhere else to turn. As such, places go, it was known as a nice place for children with a kind couple that loved children.

On one particular day, the heat had been building all day. The old folks sat around on the porches or under shade trees talking about the weather and fanning themselves trying to stay cool. Along about 4 o'clock, the weather took an ominous turn. The sky turned black as night. A cold wind began blowing up from the southwest and flickers of lightning could be seen while the crash of thunder began to rattle the windows.

The people gathered their children and got them into underground shelters if they had them. The ones who didn't got into the basements and prayed for deliverance from what they knew was coming and then suddenly there it was a monstrous black funnel swept down out of the sky churning across the plains destroying everything in its path. It was a monstrous thing and it was headed directly for the orphanage. It seemed that over 40 children and their guardians were doomed.

Then suddenly out of nowhere for no reason, a huge black cloud descended out of nowhere between the funnel and the orphanage. People that seen it said it seems that huge cloud stood there defying the funnel to come any further. At last the black monstrous funnel lifted off the ground to go back into the sky wherever it came from. The orphanage was saved. What was that huge black cloud that stopped the twister that day? I believed it was angels. You can believe what you will.

A Warning that Went Unheeded

California had long been known as the golden state. Sutter's Mill 1849 brought about the gold rush when the precious metal was discovered there.

It brought people by the hundreds of thousands from all over the world. People came from England, Iceland, France and Scandinavia. Chinese people like everyone came from China hoping to strike it rich.

People from as far away as Australia came looking to hit the big strike.

However, not every person who came there realized they were in terrible danger, from a threat that they didn't know existed.

Then one afternoon a man stopped at the sheriff's office. He had two other men with him who waited outside.

The man delivered a dire warning about a terrible calamity that would happen sometime within ten years. Many people would be consumed by fire. San Francisco would be shaken and crumble to the ground. The sheriff would later say that there was something strange about the men. Nothing he could put his finger on but something that made you listen.

The only hope was to abandon the city and move into the countryside away from destruction to come. They told the people not to reveal the source of their warning.

The trouble was no one wanted to abandon their homes and their livelihoods. Many families had lived there for years. Railroads had come to San Francisco bringing prosperity as the men of the west shipped their gold and products such as seafood east. They had learned how to use the railroad to bring into the far western cities of California people to grow fruit and cattle produce wine for the tables in the east.

Then came 1906, suddenly the ground started shaking and undulating like a living thing. Fires sprang up from everywhere. People died under tons or debris. A pall of dust hung over the city. Then as it started, the shaking stopped only to begin again over and over as aftershocks hit.

The fires continued almost everywhere. As the men had said giving the warning years before so came the Great San Francisco Earthquake of 1906. Although there have been many earthquakes since, none caused the loss of life and property damage as bad as this one. If the warnings of the visitors had been heeded, many lives might have been spared.

Such was the way of things in the west. It seems that wherever they came from, they knew many years before. It happened what was coming the question is how.

THE HANGING OF JOSE GARCIA

San Antonio Texas 1800 Just Down the Street from The Alamo

Once in a while in the history of what has come down to us and been referred to a time called the Wild West. A mystery arises that confound logic. Such is the story of the hanging of Jose Garcia. When an innocent man was about to lose his life, someone or something stepped in. In those days, almost everyone carried a gun. Mix guns, whiskey, cards, and it was an explosive combination. Many men went to the gallows when they were innocent. Case in point in one Boothill Cemetery hung by mistake in 1882.

Jose Garcia was a young Mexican boy that was around twenty or so when the story takes place. Jose wasn't really a bad boy, just full of life and loved to sing with a band around the local saloons and house parties, danced with the senoritas, and drank a little too much now and then. He carried a gun but as far as anybody knew, he had never pulled it on anyone. He worked during roundup at the local ranches and sometimes on the drives north to the railroads.

Jose did gamble a little now and then and he would win once in a while but he'd lose more often than he won. On one particular night, Jose had lost what amounted to almost a month's wages to an out of town gambler that everyone knew as a slick. Jose accused him of cheating but the gambler pulled a gun quick as a snake and told Jose to get out. Jose figured the best course of action was to leave before getting shot.

That was one of the few times Jose let his temper get away from him. He told the gambler to give his money back or he'd kill him. The next morning, the gambler was found dead. No money was on him. It really made no difference that Jose's family said he was home all night and Jose had no money on him. He was a Mexican and had threatened to kill the gambler and that was that. The jury was only out an hour. The verdict was guilty. Jose swore he was innocent but it made no difference. The Judge sentenced him to hang anyway.

For a week, Jose had to listen to the sounds of the town building his gallows. Meanwhile at Jose's home, his mother and father prayed every night for someone to help their son, a soft knock came on the door. When they opened it, a young man was standing there. They would later say that it was someone they had never seen before. But that his face and his garments shone like the sun. His words to them were, *"Fear not. It is known that your son is innocent. No one can do him harm."*

At moonrise on the last night, Jose heard them testing the gallows and he could tell the trap worked fine. Jose's parent had told him about the late night visitor to their home, but when they got him up for the march to the gallows, his courage failed him. When they placed the noose around his neck and the hood was pulled down over his face, he swore again he was innocent.

The priest said his last words, the hangman pulled the lever. Nothing happened. The trap didn't move. Again, the lever was pulled and again, the trap didn't fall. The Sheriff ordered that Jose be taken back to the jail and the hangman was to make sure the next time the gallows would fulfill its grisly task. A 200-pound sack of wheat was placed on the trap that was about what Jose weighed. The lever was pulled and the trap fell just as it was designed to do. One more try was made to hang Jose, the trap was stuck tight. Nothing could make it fall. AT LAST, HANGING Jose was given up for the rest of the day while the Sheriff and the Judge asked a higher court what to do. *"No man should have to stand on that trap between Heaven and Hell"*, the Judge said.

That night as the Sheriff was enjoying a quiet smoke after supper, a knock came on the door. When he opened it, a young man stood there. He asked to see Jose. The Sheriff would later say he usually didn't let anyone have visitors but this time he made an exception. He really didn't know what was said but after the young man left, Jose seemed to feel a lot better. Suddenly, the deputy came running in. *"You better come quick Sheriff; we got us a mess in the back of the Boarding House!"*

When the Sheriff arrived at the scene, he found a dead body. The man had killed himself. A note was pinned to his shirt, he confessed to the killing of the gambler. It seemed that he could no longer live with what Garcia was going through for what he had done and to save Garcia, he left a message before killing himself.

As for the young man that visited Jose at the jail, the Sheriffs witness that he had left him to visit Jose and Jose's parents, no trace of him leaving town on the stage of the livery. There was no proof he'd ever been in town! So goes the story of Jose Garcia. Was the young man an angel, I choose to believe he was.

Preamble to: The Old Man's Winter Night Visitor

All of us must face separation from our loved ones at death sooner or later. When a young love dies, which in the Wild West whether it came from a bullet, knife or disease; the sorrow was almost more than could be bared. Then sometimes very rarely, someone or something steps in. I choose to believe an angel was sent to the broken hearted, that this is one such story.

At the edge of one of our old western towns, stands an old house weather beaten and old, condemned now because of its age and the many years it's remained empty. Its owner was found dead one winter morning by the town's people that had come to check on him. He had frozen to death with no heat in the old house. But there was a smile upon his face.

The Old Man's Winter Night Visitor

The old timers say the winter was cold that year; the temperature hovered near forty below. The old man shivered and shook eyeing his shrinking pile of coal. The wind howled and whistled like a thing alive with a wail, like the banshee's moan. The old man signed and added to the fire, then sat down to his supper alone. For a while afterwards, he sat and smoked his pipe, lost in thoughts of more pleasant days, and he wondered just how he'd come to this old and abandoned this way.

For once, this old house was a cheery place. Children's laughter rang through the halls. Now, only the night wind sang to him and the fire, casting shadows and weird shapes upon the walls. Down in the pantry a family of mice looked at the meager fare offered there, looked at each other and shook their heads, then returned to the scraps under their stairs. A self-respecting mouse could starve to death with no more to eat than that. And if any more mice left this old house, there wouldn't be enough left to support the cat.

The wind swirled and twirled under the moonlight out on the lawn. The old house moaned and groaned, as old houses do, as the night crept on. The chill seemed to penetrate every corner as the frost seeped through the stones. The house complained as if in pain as the wind rattled its bones. The old man at last was lost in dreams of the girl that still held his heart and he smiled in his sleep dreaming of how happy they were before death tore them apart. He dreamed of warm fields of sunlight and of her laughter tinkling in the wind, and he knew he'd give all he owned just to hold her once again.

And then he felt a reassuring touch on his shoulder, the old man was no longer alone and a gentle voice said, *"John, she's waiting for you and I've come to take you home." Now the* old house still stands there weather-beaten and old, baked in the heat of summer sun, frozen by the winters cold.

Somewhere two lovers rejoice, never to be parted again. Safe in each other's arms, away from the troubles of men bodies once beat with age, again young and strong. The meadows are green, the brooks clear and deep, the meadowlark sings its song. So ends our tale of a sad winter's night and an old man broken and alone. For he's where he wanted to be for such a long time now, home!

Strange Happenings on the Trail Dodge / Ghost herd

From the Tales of Holmes Mckinisai

It was the days of the big cattle drives. Herds numbering in the thousands plodded their way north from Texas to Abilene. I was a young feller back then, all youth and fire. Not afraid of the devil. I didn't have any ties. I had lost my ma and pa to the fever and my brothers died in the war. There was nothing left in Texas, only cattle. Those long horns numbered in the millions. Everyone knew that the one thing people needed in the east was meat. Somebody got the idea of driving a herd of those old longhorns north to the railheads at Abilene Dodge and Wichita. From there the cattle buyers would ship them east.

Anyways, we'd brought in the herd and after some haggling, the boss got a dang good price. He paid us boys off and then there was some general hell raisin for three or four days. Wine, women and songs, only it wasn't wine, it was rye whiskey, strong enough to blow your hat off. I woke up the fifth morning with the worst headache I'd ever had and just enough money to see me back to Texas to be ready for the next drive north. For a young man with no ties, it was a great life.

Well anyways, rather than to spend what little money we had left a bunch of us fellas decided that we'd buy some supplies and head back to Texas the next morning. Now everything was going great. We took our time riding slow and easy, stopping about every sundown, camping along the trail. About the third night after supper, we was sitting around just talking. A couple of fellas had a card game going, just enjoying ourselves before heading for the blankets.

Anyways, we'd all turned in. I was just about asleep when the sound of a big herd goin' by on the trail woke everybody up. There was the sound of bawlin cattle shakin' of the ground, cowboy hollerin' to each other, the creakin' of the chuck wagon and it sounded like at least 3,000 head of cattle. But the next morning, not a trace. There should have been hoof prints, manure, dust and grass torn up, but nothing, absolutely nothing to show that a herd had passed. We all knew that we heard and listened too goin' by, but nothing. The only conclusion we could come to was a ghost heard. I worked on drives for the next 10 years and never heard or saw anything out of the way again.

However, I did talk to cowboys on the other drives and ranches that told of washouts that were avoided during a stampede because of a warning from somebody that showed up, gave a warning, then vanished as quick as they showed up.

Another strange story told of a bunch of rustlers that were all set to do deliberately stampede a herd. Now a herd of cattle is usually mighty spooky. They'll sometimes take off running at the drop of a hat. On this particular night drivers had the herd bedded down and were figuring on a nice quiet night. The weather was good so there was really nothing to worry about. Then all of a sudden, this huge bright light descended down over the herd. At the same time, this bunch of brush poppers started yelling and shooting off their pistols hoping to get a stampede going. Nothing happened. The cattle wouldn't run. It was like the steers couldn't hear the yelling and the guns. The light rather than scare in those old longhorns seemed to calm them. Those rustlers were scared out of their wits. The word went out that that trail was haunted for a while. After that bright light saved the herd that night, people said angels protected whoever traveled that trail, maybe so. I'm just an old man now that' made his last drive. But I did hear of some mighty strange happenings along that trail into Dodge.

Preamble to: The Men with the Tied Down Guns

They came riding in, out of the desert, keeping their backs to the sun. Seven grim men with their hats pulled low and every man wore a tied down gun. The dogs ran out in a noisy chorus then one by one they slunk away. Even the dogs knew they weren't like the other men. Tonight there'd be hell to pay. They sat their horses at the end of the street, quietly checking the town, they sat like seven angels of death making neither more nor sound.

The horses they rode were from the first to the last, all a giant of the breed, all black as the raven's wing. All huge and powerful steeds, they moved as one to the front of the saloon. Each moved like a well-oiled machine.

Hands hung close to the tied down guns, each man hard-eyed and mean. And each of us wondered what they'd come for, these men with tied down guns. We all asked question in the back of our minds, am I the reason they've come?

All afternoon they sat in the saloon, each with his back to the wall watchin' every move in the place. Seeing if one of us would "*Open the ball.*" The leader of the bunch was the biggest of all, at least six foot five or more. He spoke not a word and only his eyes moved, watching the windows and doors. His face was cold and hard. His eyes glittered under his hat, only the devil himself on his throne in hell ever had a look like that. The heat hung over the street like a shroud so hot it threatened to bludgeon you dumb. Mothers kept the kids in off the street. Fearing at nightfall death would come. And you know there was some kinda smell hung in the air, kinda like a fog filling the skies. Felt like it could choke off your bread. The smell of it burning your eyes, kinda like black powder smoke, but somehow stronger still.

Down in the street everything was quiet as death; the sun, sunken behind the hills. The preacher called us into the church and boy the place was filled to the doors. The pews were full and so were the aisles, children were crouching on the floors. And Benny the drunk vowed to never drink again, not even to help his cough. And Tommy Steele, the town's tough kid dropped his gun in the water. Tough men shook hands with their neighbors, forgetting disagreements they'd had before and a man wanted for twenty years gave up at the jailhouse door. Then the clock on the courthouse struck making us jump out our skins, making us feel it was the stroke of doom. Then the preacher led us in prayer again. And while we sat there in the church waiting for hell to start out in the street, the fires of perdition feeling so close, we could almost feel the heat. Then the sound of galloping hoof beats headed for the edge of town. Seven men on seven horses headed away, what a beautiful sound.

Then the preacher started chucklin' down deep in his chest and all the rest of us joined in slapping our knees and wiping our eyes, the town comin' alive again. And the smell of fire and brimstone no longer burned our eyes. The moon rose in majestic beauty into a cloudless sky.

Who were they that visited us on that day so long ago? Were they lawmen, were they outlaws? Nobody seems to know! But they sure made a change in our town, these men with the tied down guns. Were they visitors from heaven or a warning from hell, nobody knew from whence they'd come you know. Benny died an old, old man who no longer had his cough. And for years afterward, you could see a rusted Six Gun at the bottom of the water trough. Well boy, you ask me if this stories true. Damn right. I was there when the devil sat on a barstool and fire and brimstone filled the air. The church filled up for the very first time when they came, riding in out of the sun. Every one of us breathed a lot easier when they left, these men with the tied down guns.

The Last Citizen of Dry Creek

From the Pen of Big Irv Lampman 2020

It was like a lot of those towns where in those days the mines were closed so its reason for existing was gone so it had dried up and was withering away! The saloon was home now to the bats and owls and an occasional coyote that came wandering by, all in all was a miserable place, this dry creek town! I had little time so I went exploring.

A feller never knew what he might run across in a place that dried up and old. Might even find some silver coins or even a poke of gold. There wasn't much! The bats, owls, and foxes had staked their claim to all of it. You know the sad part was it was a nice place before the mines played out, what a shame!

In the jail, he sheriff's office was just about the worst thing I'd ever seen! In the jail locked in one cells was a skeleton of a man! But he wasn't supposed to be there, got locked in by accident so it seems! On a brown piece of paper, he'd scribbled a note that read, "I was just going to spend the night but the door slammed shut behind and now 3 months later, I'm dead! I haven't found the keys to the cell, the ghost of the sheriff comes by! He don't pay attention to me though I bang on the bars with this old tin cup some body drank coffee out of a year ago. Well, it won't be long now and I'll be joinin' him I guess! So here I am, the last citizen of dry creek!"

The Unbelievable Prediction of Crazy Horse

From the Pen of Big Irv Lampman 2012

Crazy Horse as almost everyone knows was the great war chief that defeated Custer at the battle of The Little Big Horn in 1876. What most people don't know is that Crazy Horse made two predictions. First, that he would be killed by his own people which came true! He was killed by his own people! But then came the most incredible prediction of all! He said, "The day will come when I will return to my people in stone!"

Right now on Mount Rushmore joining Washington, Lincoln, Roosevelt and Thomas Jefferson, the statue of Crazy Horse is being carved on the mountain! He has returned to his people in stone!

The Legend of Colter's Hell

From the Pen of Big Irv Lampman 2016

One of the greatest mountain men if not the greatest was Jim Bridger, but along with his other major accomplishments was his ability to tell tall tales and stretch the truth a mile! For example, he told of being surrounded by a black foot war party and after 4 days of fierce fisting, he said he ran out of powder and ball and black feet closed in!

"Well, what happened, Jim?"

"Well they killed me of course!"

Jim Bridger was classed of the greatest teller of tall tales ever but then one day, John Colter spoke up! "I found a place in the mountains where it can be thirty below and there's places where there's hot tubs of stone where you can jump in and the water's warm as toast! Huge geysers of steam boil out of the ground! You can pull fish out of the springs already boiled and ready to eat! There's buffalo and grizzly everywhere and there's wood on the ground ready to cut up for firewood!"

One of the other mountain men spoke up and said, "You've finally been bested by a better teller of tales! Jim, you can't beat it!" and so it was thought to be a tall tale! Now, we call Colter's Hell, Yellow Stone Park!

The Tale of the Walker - Bennesh Wagon Train and the Desert Crossing

From the Pen of Big Irv Lampman

One of the most dreaded problem of the wagon trains headed west to the bold fields in California was the lack of water, both for the people and their animals, horses, and oxens. In this particular story, the Walker-Bennesh train, they had been struggling to reach a small river that was running through a valley where there would be plenty of water for the animals and fresh water to drink and for the women to cook with and fill the water barrels. The trouble was, the river was dry. Only dust was there to offer the thirsty travelers.

Now, the people were facing death from thirst and starvation. It was decided to send out scouts to try and locate another source of fresh water, but as it had been an especially dry year. The wagon master didn't hold out much hope, but he decided to keep the threat from the travelers as long as he could.

On the fourth night, things were getting desperate! Thirst was taking its toll on the grown-ups and the children were suffering greatly.

The scouts returned around sundown with no water to be found anywhere. The train had reconciled to a slow death! Just as the sun dipped below the horizon, the sounds of hoof beats were heard and the creaking of harnessers could be heard. When the wagons pulled into the firelight, the slushing of water in water kegs was apparent or all to have enough water for the people, the animals and plenty left over to fill the water barrels. The people said that despite their rugged appearance, the men driving looked incredibly like angels. That night, it started to rain and by morning, the

Angels and Mysteries and Incredible Happenings in the Wild Wild West

river was running fresh and clean. The angels, for that's what the people on the train believed that's what they were said they would guide the train across the deserts and make sure they would make it through all right. The little river continues to flow fresh and clean to these days. So goes our tale of the angels and the wagon train.

The Saving of Boonesborough

From the Pen of Big Irv Lampman

The settlement of Boonesboough in Kentucky in the 1700's had been under siege from Chief Blackfish and his Shawne Warriors for a week. After many attempts to breach the walls and a cost of many of his warriors' lives, the Indians had devised a plan to set fire to the wooden stockade with fire arrows. The stockade and the roof of the Blackhouse was afire!

The minister has taken the women and children into the church to wait for what they thought would be a terrible bloody death! Boone Jacob Wetzel and Simon Kenton had prepared the Frontiersmen to fight to the last man. The minister and the women were praying, and suddenly the sky turned black as night and a tremendous storm came up! It drowned out the fire in the stockade and the Blockhouse! It drowned out the Indians' fires and drenched the fields so that the pioneers couldn't get in the fields for two weeks. Chief Blackfish said he believed Boonesborough was protected by the great spirit and never attacked Boone and his little settlement ever again! I choose to believe the Great Spirit saved Boonesborough and the little group of pioneers because of the faith of the minister and the little group of people gathered in prayer in the church.

The Legend of Wyatt Earp: The Man No Bullet Could Kill

From the Pen of Big Irv Lampman

In the history of the wild west, one name stands out, Wyatt Earp; town tamer, gun fighter, lawman, marshal - all of them at different times described Wyatt Earp. The one fight he was involved in a long with his brothers, Morgan and Virgil, was the most famous gunfights of all the gunfights at the O.K. Corral at Tombstone, Arizona. On Oct. 26, 1881 against the Clantons and McClaurys, three men killed and three men hurt in 30 seconds! The only man left standing was Wyatt Earp.

Later at Iron Spring Curly Bill Brocious fired point blank at Wyatt Earp with a shotgun, Wyatt's clothes were full of holes, his hat was shot off along with a boot heel, but again, Wyatt was untouched and killed Curly Bill. Wyatt Earp lived to be an old man and died in Los Angeles in 1929, truly the man no bullet could kill.

Could it be for some reason the angels protected Wyatt Earp for some reasons?

Geronimo: The Businessman

From the Pen of Big Irv Lampman

Geronimo was best known as the War Chief of the Apache Indians until his capture and removal to another area. However, he also become for those days a rich man. One day as he got off his train, some of the tourists asked him to buy the buttons off so they could say they owned the buttons off Geronimo's jacket. From that time on, Geronimo would buy buttons, sow them on his jacket, sell them to the next group of tourists and then repeat process sometimes two or three times a day. When Geronimo died, he had $10,000 in the bank, an incredible sum for those days.

The Wrong Man, The Mystery of the Death of Billy the Kid

From the Pen of Big Irv Lampman

July 14, 1881, at Fort Sumner, New Mexico, Pat Garret, the sheriff of Lincoln County had come to Fort Sumner looking for the young outlaw William Bonney, otherwise known as Billy the Kid. Garret was sitting on the bed of Pete Maxwell when who walks in but The Kid. Garret fired twice supposedly hitting The Kid in the heart killing him, but now, the story takes on the ere of mystery.

Garret's Deputy, Deputy John Poe came in with a lantern and holding it over the face of the corpse exclaimed, "You've shot the wrong man!" The body was that of a dark skinned man, dark hair and eyes and measuring five foot 8".

Billy was light complexed with blue eyes measuring 5 foot 3' and his hair was blonde. Garret hurried up and had the corpse buried at sunrise getting several witnesses to say it was The Kid's body! Garret collected 5,000 in bounty and that should have been that. The problem was, Billy wouldn't stay buried. People that knew him said he was working on a ranch in Wyoming. Buffalo Bill swore he asked Billy to join his wild west show but the The Kid was afraid that some of his old enemies from The Lincoln County war would come looking for him so The Kid decided to stay buried.

But the question remains who was it Garret shot dead on July 14, 1881? We'll probably never know.

Old Guzzler

From the Pen of Big Irv Lampman 2014

Now, no one knows how that old pony acquired his taste for beer, we only know that right after delivering 2500 head of cattle to the cattle buyers and stock pens those young wild cowboys were ready to cut loose the wolf as the saying went. A whole group of them pulled up the nearest saloon, yelling and firing their sixguns into the air.

One of the men rode on his horse into the saloon and put a gallon of beer down on the floor in front of him. That old bronc inhaled that gallon big time and was looking around for more, then every cowboy wanted to buy the old pony a beer.

The old horsie lapped them up! Somebody said, "Another drink for old Guzzler!" And the name stuck, and from that time on whenever his rider hit town, old Guzzler waited patiently outside until his rider brought out a 5-gallon pail of beer and Guzzler took his time enjoying it. And it was said when all that green grass and beer would mix inside of him, you wouldn't want to be anywhere near. We used to smear beer up around his eyes and watch that tongue of his come out and his eyes would cross in a look of pure enjoyment. Well, all good things must end, I'm sure when his time came it was in a pasture of green grass, surrounded by pretty little mares and the smell of dandelions. And if he's in there somewhere and we meet at The Great Saloon in the sky, I'll be proud to buy him a gallon cold one!

THE SPEECH OF CHIEF LOGAN

From the Pen of Big Irv Lampman 2014

For the most part in the latter part of 1700's, the Indians were classed as ignorant savages with not one redeeming feature. However, the Indians were the greatest natural orator to be found anywhere, case in point Chief Logan.

I asked my white brother when did he come to Logan Village, hungry and thirsty, and his needs were not tended. *When did he come naked and was not clothed or when did he come wounded and bleeding and his wounds were not bound up? When was he not shown kindness?*

During the last bloody war, I didn't make war and remained in my village. The other warriors and chiefs said, "Logan is a friend to the white man", and so I was.

A few years ago while I was away hunting soldiers under colonel Cresap attacked my village and killed my wife, my children and my mother and father. There runs not one drop of Logan blood in any living creature. Logan has made war. I have glutted my vengeance.

Now, I am sick of war! I will make war no more! But not from fear, Logan has never felt fear. Who is now there to mourn for Logan? Not one!

Abilene Kansas, "Hell Has Laid Its Egg and at Abilene it Hatched"

From the Pen of Big Irv Lampman 2014

Abilene, Kansas in the 1880's was the railhead where the cattle drives from Texas was paid for and put on cattle cars to be shipped east to feed the eastern cities.

After 4 months or more on the drive, the young cowboys were full of pent up energy, and where's there is whiskey and guns and soiled doves in the mix there was hell to pay. The city fathers got together and hired the toughest town tamer they knew of, James Butler Hickock better known as "Wild Bill". Hickock was the only man able to put a lid on the town and keep it there. Of course, Wild Bill wasn't like most of the town tamers of his day.

Wyatt Earp said, "A dead man can't buy more whiskey or patronize the stores or soiled doves!"

Hickock didn't give a damn. He was just as liable to shoot a man as look at him. He put the fear of God into drovers that came to Abilene.

But Bill's career came to a screechin' halt one night. A local tough named Phil Coe was shooting his gun around the town one night and Bill called him on it. Coe drew on Hickock and Wild Bill killed him. Just then Mike Williams, the deputy came running up behind Hickock calling Bill, Hickock whirled and killed his own deputy.

The town fathers decided that Wild Bill was too wild even for Abilene. They decided not to renew Bill's contract, Hickock never wore a badge again. He drifted through the west and was finally shot and killed by Jack McCall, a little snot that wasn't fit to lick Bill's Boots. Bill was buried in the Deadwood Cemetery and then moved to Mt. Moriah cemetery.

Later, Calamity Jane asked to be buried next to Wild Bill and so she was. It had been said that Wild Bill probably hasn't had a wink of rest or quiet night since.

The Wonderful Christmas Story in Wyoming 1891

From the Pen of Big Irv Lampman 2010

Christmas in Wyoming that year began like any other. It was decided by the city fathers that a Christmas pageant would be put on and for that purpose, a traveling show of actors and actress would be hired to produce and act in the show. The children were in a hurry for Christmas morning and the grown-ups were excited to see the show.

The evening of the big show arrived. A few sheep and some goats and two or three cows were in pens for the children to pet and make over. Mary and Joseph took their places and the show began. The three wise men came to take their place and after the show was over, the old man with the red suit, big belly and white beard showed up to the delight of the children to pass out presents. Finally, the night was over and the people put on their coats and hats and mittens for the ride home.

Just then the man from the traveling show came in with a very puzzled look on his face. "What's the matter?" the mayor asked.

"I just got a message that my 3 wise men and Santa Claus were stuck in Minnesota". They said the train derailed and they can't get here until tomorrow. "I don't understand it, who were the 3 wise men and Santa Claus?" It remains a mystery to this day. Angels is the only answer.

THE MYSTERY OF THE DODGE CITY STAGE

From the Pen of Big Irv Lampman 2017

One of the greatest mystery in the transportation industry in the wild west comes to us from Dodge City, now this stage in particular was headed from Dodge City to Wichita. It was carrying around $25,000 in gold in a hidden safe under the driver's box and 5 passengers, 2 men, 2 women and a child, a boy about 8 years of age.

The stage pulled out for Wichita about six in the morning. Everything must have went well as the stage stopped on time at bonners station to change horses, grab a bite to eat and then pulled out for the next leg of the trip.

Nothing was ever heard from the stage again, not of the passengers, or the gold, or the driver. Nothing! The United States Marshal, Bat Masterson and his Deputy led a posse to comb the canyons, the prairies coolies and the settler's cabins, nothing! A group of Indians was asked if they had seen or heard anything about the stage and they didn't believe the stage would ever be found. And so it remains to this day, the mysterious disappearance of the Dodge City Stage.

Marshall Taylor's Last Day

From the Pen of Big Irv Lampman 2011

Marshal Sam Taylor checked his gun as he always did before stepping out on the boardwalk in front of the jail. Not that the marshall was looking for trouble, this was the marshall's last day before retirement with nothing to do but sit on the porch and tell stories of the Wild West to the neighborhood boys that might wander by, and the marshall had lots of stories to tell.

He'd been a mountain man, Indian fighter and a fast gun in his day, but now, there were too many white hairs showing under his hat and he had to admit he wasn't as fast as he once was. Mary, his wife said it was time to put away the badge and let a younger man have it, as for the gun, well, he'd carry that for a while. As a matter of fact, he'd feel downright naked without it.

Just then, Tom, his Deputy came running in the door.

"Marshall, the Burnsten Gang is headed this way! A telegraph just came from Hadley Ville! They robbed the bank there and killed two men! Now, they're headed our way!"

"Tom, call a meeting of the town fathers!" the Marshall said. "I need to get some help", he added.

But the city fathers declined to get in a gunfight with a gang of outlaws as vicious as the Burnstens Gang. In the history of the west, those men were just about the most vicious during the Civil War. They had been raiders all over Kansas and Missouri and some of the men had ridden with Quantrill's raiders.

Mary wanted the marshall to put the badge on the marshall's desk and just walk away, but Taylor wasn't built that way. This had been his town for years and on his last day in office, he wasn't about to turn it over to a bunch of murderers and cutthroats, no sir!

The old lawmen loaded up two Winchesters, a shotgun and a belt full of cartridges and sat on the chair in front of the Marshall's office waiting for hell to ride in. He didn't have long to wait.

A band of fifteen men rode in and stopped in front of the bank. Men went in while the rest waited outside. Just as the men came out of the bank with money in hand, suddenly men with rifles appeared everywhere on rooftops, out of the windows and the corners of buildings all up and down the street.

"You men had best drop your weapons and give it up now. You're not gonna ride out of this town alive if you make a fight of it!" the men shouted.

"We're here to back up Marshall Taylor! We fully intend to lock you up or plant you in Boot Hill, it's your choice!"

There were some tense moments then but the outlaws dropped their weapons and surrendered! The Marshall locked them up, dropped his badge on the desk in the Marshall's office and went home to Mary, but when he went out to thank the men who had came and helped him, not a man could be found! No one had seen them ride in or ride out. So, who were they? It remains a mystery to this day, only God knows what happened on Marshall Taylor's last day.

LION

From the Pen of Big Irv Lampman 2011

This story comes from the trail up from Texas to Abilene from an old puncher that swore it was true. The old man's time on the cattle for free gazing was a thing of the past. Anyway, here's the story just as he told it to me in his own words!

"We'd been traveling along pretty good!" The herd had been plodding along their way north to the railhead where they would be put on boxcars for their way east to the slaughterhouse in the east to feed the people that needed meat for their families. On this particular night that I'm speaking of the cook had just served up the bacon and beans when this God awful roarin' started in. It wasn't like a bear or mountain lion, it was deep down in the throat of whatever it was a terrible groanin' like I'd never heard before. The herd was on its feet and movin' in about 3 seconds and the horses was goin' crazy and then took off Haulin' Hooves as fast as they could for other parts.

"I don't mind tellin' you I was feelin' a might skittish myself!"

"I'd spent 20 years lookin' over a herd of longhorns and fightin' dust, tornadoes, Comanche's and rustlers. And I'd never heard anything like that!"

"Well, we'd have finally got the herd stopped and rounded up what we could find of our saddle stock!"

"What we found in the next morning made every one of us check our Winchesters and sixguns and made us look over our shoulders!"

"We found what was left of a steer all torn to pieces!"

"Now, I'll tell you it takes something' pretty powerful to pull down a thousand-pound longhorn like that!"

"And there was pug marks but bigger than any mountain lion I'd ever seen!"

A couple of the boys scouted around and followed those tracks into the hills and that was as far as they wanted to follow them. I guess they figured whatever could pull down a thousand-pound longhorn could pull down a man easy as that.

Of course, we had our 44-40 Winchester and the cook had a shotgun and a 45-70 under the seat but who knows if he'd ever get the chance to use it. Well, anyways, we left a couple of the boys with their Winchesters and the cooks 45-70 watchin' the kill site. I figured if the thing was like any other cat it would return to the kill to Gorge itself, if it did, we'd be waitin'.

That night we'd just got settled down and had doubled upon the nighthawks singin' their heads off tryin' to keep the herd settled down when that awful groanin' roar started up.

"I'm tellin' you, my hair just stood up, trying to poke holes in my hat!"

I had never heard anything like it and judging by the way they acted, neither had the horses. It was all we could do to keep our whole damn remuda from taken off back to Texas. I cocked my Winchester 44-40 and eared back the hammer on my 45 side gun and wished I was back in Texas, but I wasn't, so there was no use wishin'.

Anyways, the thing didn't make another killing that night, maybe it had a feeling that we were layin' for him and was just watchin' its chance to take one of us. I figured it was bound to get one of us sooner or later.

The next morning, I heard Jimmy, the cook's helper let a yell out of him that would raise the dead. We came up out of our blankets with rifles and sixguns cocked and ready. It's a dang good thing nobody got shot with a yell like that. Jimmy's eyes were buggin' out and he was pointin' at the ground. There was those big pug marks where the thing had walked around and around the camp wantin' to take one of us but not quite ready to do it. That cook's helper was scared to death and I don't blame him. There was a 500-pound cat out there, a killer of livestock and maybe men. I had no doubt the thing would take a man if he could get away with it.

We got the herd movin' and made about 10 miles that day. I hoped we'd left the cat behind us but no such luck.

That night the moon had just came up when a terrible scream from one of the nighthawks and roar came from out in the brush and that was all. We grabbed our rifles and some lanterns and went out to where Pedro was supposed to be. All we found was a horse with a broken neck and trail of blood leading out into the dark brush. There wasn't a man amongst us who wouldn't help Pedro if we thought we could help but no man could lose that much blood and live. And there was no sense losing another man going out into the dark after that thing.

The other hands had their 44:40's and I had the cooks 45-70, but it was what they used to call a trap door model and it was single shot and if you didn't kill with the first shot, you were in trouble cause sometimes you had to dig out the empty before you could reload. More than one fella got eaten by a grizzly because of that.

Anyways, I had to send one of the boys into town for the sheriff cause even in those days there had to be an inquest. They got back around 3 in the afternoon. The sheriff looked around and the doctor looked over the killin' sight and finally he told us that we weren't the first drive to tangle with this cat. A rancher had gone out to check on a line shack and found both of the lineriders dead and the whole corral of horses just tore to pieces. There were big pug prints all over, there was no doubt about it.

One of his older hands had been to Africa on Safari and he'd heard that thing roarin' and he said no doubt was there. That thing was an African Lion but what in Hell was it doin' in Texas bedevilin' cattle drives. Nobody could answer that question. The old fella had gone to Africa with a rich man that wanted to go to Africa and hired the old hand to go with him. The sheriff said when that old driver said something you could take it to the bank. Another young fella was headed back to the home place after sparkin's his sweetheart in town when all of a sudden his horse went crazy and took off with the young driver hangin' on for dear life. Something had scared that horse out of his mind.

The next morning, the young fella and a couple of his friends loaded down with heavy rifles went out to where his horse had went crazy and found these big tracks all around. I guess nobody thought to tell that kid just how lucky he was to see sunrise. If his horse hadn't bolted, he most likely would have been filling some big cat's belly in the morning.

Well, the sheriff got his paperwork filled out, the doctor did his and headed back to town. That night was Saturday so I let some of the fellas off to go to town. I'd hired some extra hands with Winchesters to help guard the herd. I'd made up my mind that if that damn cat wanted to take another steer or to kill one of my riders, it was goin' to cost him. I loaded up the cooks 45-70. Put extra shell in my pockets made sure my 45 was ready for whatever came along and settled down to wait. The moon came up and sailed high into the heavens, there was a little breeze came up and it fanned the fire under the roast beef the cook had goin' for the crew to eat the next day. Then something I couldn't put my finger on it, made the hairs on the back of my neck stand up and take notice. Then all of a sudden I could smell this strong musty odor that said "cat". Then I heard this heavy breathin' and a deep rumblin' growl and I knew.

That about a minute or so from then I'd have 500 pounds of teeth and claws on my back and be torn to shreds. I tried to bring the 45-70 around but every move I made brought the thing closer to a charge. I said my prayers and figured I's be dead in a minute or so and then for whatever reason, the thing was gone. My legs wouldn't hold me. I'd been near death and I hung onto that old 45-70 like I was married to it. I couldn't understand why I wasn't dead. I still can't! Maybe the thing got a whiff on one of the men coming back and didn't like the odds, I don't know.

Well anyways, that's the story. The herd moved on toward Abilene and that was the last I had anything to do with that lion. I did hear that a circus train had derailed around there somewhere and that must have been where that critter came from. Anyways, that's the story of the lion. Some ranchers and cowhand seen or heard it later but that's all I know.

When the Buffalo Came Back

From the Pen of Irv Lampman

Jim Bridger, the mountain man was well known as a spinner of tall tales, but there was one story he told that he swore was absolutely true. The Sioux, Cheyenne and Black Foot Tribes had sworn to wipe the white men out of the Black Hill and the Rocky Mountains. The reason was the killing of the Buffalo to the point of no return. The Indian depended on the buffalo for food, shelter, clothing in winter, weapons and just about everything.

Bridger, Kit Carson and the other mountain men knew that should the tribes unite the tribes would then be strong enough to destroy Bridger's trading post, several of the forts in the West. Chief sitting Bull and Crazy Horse were preparing for war. Bridger said a meeting among the mountain men had been told by the Indian the only way war could be prevented was the buffalo must return so that the tribes could make it through till spring. The white men knew that was impossible. The Great Plains were strewn with carcasses and bleaching bones.

However, the Indians told a strange tale. Supposedly a great shining light had over shown the main village and three men in garment s that shown as bright as the sun came from the light and told the tribes the Buffalo would return for one final time that summer. However, the tribes would have hard times for a while. The buffalo would survive in a small herd and slowly come back. The tribes could hunt that fall but that was all. A few days later, the scouts reported that as had been told to them a great herd of buffalo had appeared in a valley on the Great Plains, enough to feed and clothe them for winter. The stranger had told the tribes that they must not make war or the buffalo would vanish as quickly as they had appeared. As was foretold, the buffalo did survive and in later years has made a wonderful come back. Who were these men that came from the light and brought back the buffalo? I believe they were angels. There can be no other explanation. Had not the heavenly visitors intervened the war between the Indians and the White Mountain Men would have devastated both sides. Thank God it didn't happen!

"And so we say goodbye to this version of Angels and Mysteries and Incredible Happenings in the Wild West! There are more stories that I may tell someday."

Best Wishes,
Irv Lampman

www.ingramcontent.com/pod-product-compliance
Lightning Source LLC
LaVergne TN
LVHW060216080526
838202LV00052B/4287